W9-AMO-868

# The
# Cuckoo-Clock
# Cuckoo

# The Cuckoo-Clock Cuckoo

by Annegert Fuchshuber

Carolrhoda Books, Inc./Minneapolis

This edition copyright © 1988 by
Carolrhoda Books, Inc. All rights reserved.

Original edition © 1982 by Sellier Verlag GmbH, Eching bei
München, West Germany under the title KUCKUCKS-UHR-KUCKUCK.

Library of Congress Cataloging-in-Publication Data

Fuchshuber, Annegert.
  The cuckoo-clock cuckoo.

  Translation of: Kuckucks-uhr-kuckuck.
  Summary: Follow the adventures of a cuckoo-clock
cuckoo who, after escaping from his clock, finds that
he can't get back in.
[ 1. Cuckoos—Fiction. 2. Clocks and watches—
Fiction ] I. Title.
PZ7.F94Cu   1988      [E]        87-30950
ISBN 0-87614-320-6 (lib. bdg.)

Manufactured in the United States of America

1  2  3  4  5  6  7  8  9  10  98  97  96  95  94  93  92  91  90  89  88

# The Cuckoo-Clock Cuckoo

**12:00 A.M.**

It was midnight, and the Zeitler family was sound asleep. The clock in the church tower bonged twelve times. Then the cuckoo bird in the Zeitlers' cuckoo clock called out "Cuckoo" twelve times.

The house was all quiet and dark. Then, through an open window, the cuckoo saw a fluffy white something fluttering about.

"Hello," whispered the fluffy something.

"Hello," croaked the cuckoo. "Who are you?"

"I'm a ghost," answered the shadowy creature. "Why don't you come out and play?"

The cuckoo wasn't sure he could do that, but he spread his wooden wings and flapped them hard. Clumsily, he flew across the kitchen to the windowsill.

Outside, a whole band of ghosts romped about in the moonlight. Up and down they floated in a soundless dance.

"Join us!" they called out to the cuckoo.

The little cuckoo flew through the air as swift as an arrow. What fun it was to be able to fly!

**1:00 A.M.**

It was time for the cuckoo to return to his clock and announce the hour! Quickly he flew toward the clock—and unexpectedly bumped his head on the closed door. Confused, the little cuckoo fluttered around the kitchen. But every time he tried to get into his clock, he bumped his head.

**2:00 A.M.**

Sadly the cuckoo sat atop his clock. No matter what he tried, he couldn't get inside. He hoped the door would open when the next hour came. But at two o'clock, the clock just crackled a little. The door stayed shut. What was the little cuckoo to do?

**3:00 A.M.**

The clock in the church tower struck three. The cuckoo rattled his wings and tried to call out "Cuckoo" three times. But the only sound he could make was a hoarse croak. Was this the end of his cuckoo-clock life? Could anybody hear him?

The cuckoo fluttered to the windowsill. "Hey, moon," he called up at the sky. "Did you hear me?" But the moon didn't answer.

The little bird flew out to the front garden, where a flower softly gleamed in the moonlight.

"Hello, flower," the cuckoo twittered. "Did you hear me call exactly three times?" But the flower didn't answer, either.

At last the cuckoo flew to a nearby tree. In the tree sat a large owl.

"Did you hear me call?" the cuckoo asked.

"Yes, I heard you," rasped the owl. "I'm hungry, and you sound like just the right snack for me."

As fast as he could, the frightened cuckoo flew back to his safe kitchen. He looked at the clock, hoping the door might have opened by itself. But it was still closed.

**4:00 A.M.**

When four o'clock came, the door stayed shut. Now the cuckoo began to feel something strange— a growling and rumbling inside him that was new and different. He felt he *had* to find something to put into his beak—and quickly.

When his hunger grew greater than his fear of the owl, the cuckoo flew outside again. Morning was coming, but no one was out on the street yet. A light shone in a neighboring building, and the cuckoo flew toward it.

**4:02 A.M.**

What the cuckoo found was a baker hard at work making rolls. Next to the baker's oven sat a basket full of wonderful-smelling bread and buns. The growling in the cuckoo's stomach grew stronger, and he cheeped pitifully.

The baker looked up from his work and laughed. "What a strange bird you are! Would you like something to eat?"

The man spread some golden crumbs on the windowsill, and the cuckoo ate them greedily. When he was full, the wooden bird chirped a thank-you and flew away.

**6:00 A.M.**

Now the cuckoo felt much better. His fear was gone, his hunger was gone, and he was not so alone anymore. Through open windows, he heard alarm clocks ring and sleepy voices murmur. A man started to sweep off the sidewalk, and delivery trucks rushed down the street.

The Zeitler family was already in their kitchen. Father, Mother, and Susi were eating breakfast. Peter was looking for a lost sock.

**6:55 A.M.**

"Hurry up, Peter," Mother called. "It's almost seven o'clock."

Soon the clock in the church tower struck the hour. But all the Zeitlers' cuckoo clock did was rattle. Father went over to the clock, pulled on the weights, and tried to open the little door.

"Peter!" he shouted. "What did you do to the clock?"

"It wasn't me," said Peter.

"Strange," Father muttered. "Not a good start for the day."

**7:30 A.M.**

At seven-thirty, Father put down his newspaper, picked up his briefcase, and went to his office.

After the children finished breakfast, they left for school.

The curious cuckoo followed Peter and Susi to the school yard. Startled by the noisy play of all the children, the wooden bird watched from a big chestnut tree.

**8:00 A.M.**

At eight o'clock sharp, the school doors opened, and the children went inside. It became so quiet that the cuckoo was bored. He flew to an open window and saw Susi standing beside a desk in a classroom.

"Well, Susi," the teacher was saying, "do you know the answer? What bird lays its eggs in another bird's nest?"

Susi blushed. She peeked at the girl next to her, who shrugged. Then she looked out the window and saw—

"The cuckoo!" Susi blurted out.

"Very good," said the teacher. "That's right."

A little confused, Susi quickly sat down. When she looked out the window again, there was nothing to see but blue sky.

**9:00 A.M.**

When Susi had looked at the cuckoo, he had zoomed away to hide in the chestnut tree. As long as no one noticed him, maybe his trip out of the clock would stay a secret.

**10:00 A.M.**

The cuckoo decided to stay away from the school. He flew back to the street, which was now full of people. The postman delivered the mail. Shoppers bought bread at the bakery. Motorcycles and cars roared past.

The cuckoo looked into all the open windows, poked his wooden beak into steaming cooking pots, and escaped from a noisy vacuum cleaner. Finally, he landed back on the Zeitlers' windowsill.

**11:37 A.M.**

Peter and Susi were home from school to eat lunch.

"Do you think our cuckoo has flown away?" Susi asked.

"That's nonsense," said Mother. "The cuckoo is made of wood, and it's fastened to the clock. The little door is probably just jammed."

Susi tried to explain what had happened at school. "The teacher asked me a question, and I looked out the window, and I saw—Look! There it is again!"

Mother looked out the window, then shook her head. "You're imagining things, Susi. There's no cuckoo there."

When Susi spotted him for the second time, the cuckoo ducked into the flowerpot on the windowsill. He was tired and worried and homesick. He just wanted to be back inside his own clock. The Zeitlers might even get a new cuckoo for the clock. Then he would never be able to go home!

**1:00 P.M.**

As long as the family was in the kitchen eating lunch, the cuckoo didn't dare move. He tried hard not to tremble.

But Minka the cat had been staring at the flowerpot and had seen the leaves move. She decided there must be something hidden there. All at once, she jumped on the flowerpot and caught the cuckoo in her jaws. When she bit him hard, she got a terrible surprise. With a shocked *meow*, she dropped the bird into the grass below the window. All her teeth hurt from biting the wooden cuckoo.

"Minka!" shouted all the Zeitlers.

"You naughty cat!" scolded Mother. "You ruined my beautiful flowers!"

"It's a good thing I'm made of wood!" the cuckoo thought happily. Then he checked to see what harm the cat had done to him. All he could find was one small scratch. Next he tried a tiny somersault in the air. His wings still worked fine.

**3:00 P.M.**

Suddenly he saw Peter and Susi come out of the house. Peter was carrying the cuckoo clock. What was happening? The cuckoo followed the children to the building next door, where he saw many clocks in the front window. While he waited for Peter and Susi to come out, the weather changed. Dark clouds filled the sky. A gust of wind swept along the street and knocked the cuckoo over.

Terrified, the wooden bird closed his eyes tightly as thunder rumbled above him and rain poured down on him. He thought it might be the end of the world!

**4:45 P.M.**

Finally the storm passed. When the cuckoo peeked out from under his wing, he saw a bright rainbow in the sky. The door of the clock shop stood open. The cuckoo didn't see Peter or Susi inside, so he quickly hopped through the doorway.

The shop was full of clocks. There were kitchen clocks, alarm clocks, pocket watches, grandfather clocks, wristwatches—and even cuckoo clocks!

Right away, the cuckoo saw his own clock on a table. The clockmaker was bending over it.

**5:00 P.M.**

When he heard the children coming back, the cuckoo hid in a chest full of clock parts. He heard Susi ask, "Will the cuckoo ever come out of our clock again?"

"Of course he will," said the clockmaker. "He certainly can't fly away. The little door is just jammed. I don't have time to work on it today. You take the clock home with you and bring it back to me next week. The door might even unstick itself by then.

**6:00 P.M.**

After the children went home, the cuckoo sat in a tree. "That clockmaker doesn't know anything! Of course I can fly!" And to prove it, he flew up the street.

Evening was coming. People came home from work. Lamps were lit in windows, and television sets flickered on.

At the Zeitler house, Father sat in the kitchen and read his newspaper. The cat perched on the windowsill and stared angrily at the flowerpot. Upstairs, Mother helped Peter and Susi with their homework. Suddenly Susi went and put a piece of chocolate on the window ledge.

"What's that for?" asked Mother.

"It's for our cuckoo," Susi explained. "Maybe he'll come back for the candy."

"That's silly!" said Peter. "The cuckoo can't fly!"

Mother laughed. "Well, if the clockmaker can't help, maybe Susi's chocolate can."

**7:00 P.M.**

From outside, the cuckoo eyed the chocolate. He wanted it, but it would be safer to get it when the children were asleep.

**8:00 P.M.**

At eight o'clock, Peter and Susi went to bed. When he was sure they were asleep, the cuckoo felt brave enough to fly up and get the piece of candy. He looked in at the children. The cuckoo was tired, too. If only he could get into his clock so he could rest.

Downstairs, Father walked out of the house, and the cuckoo swooped to follow him. Father went to a building a little way down the street. There he joined a lot of people at a noisy meeting.

**9:00 P.M.**

As he watched the people get ready to go home after their meeting, the cuckoo began to feel frightened. He thought he could see owl eyes staring at him from the dark trees. On the sidewalk, Minka kept an eye on him and purred, "Just wait, bird. I'll get you yet!"

When someone came walking down the street, the cuckoo boldly jumped onto the man's big hat.

**10:30 P.M.**

The man in the hat behaved very strangely. He tiptoed around the neighborhood, turning door handles and peering through windows. When some-one passed by, the man ducked into the shadows, as if he didn't want to be seen.

At last the man came to a window that was familiar to the cuckoo. It was the Zeitlers' kitchen window. The cuckoo fluttered inside and was surprised when the man followed him through the window (knocking over the flowers as he climbed in).

The man turned on his flashlight and looked around the kitchen. Then he opened all the drawers and searched through them. The little cuckoo, who had never in his life seen a burglar, watched the man.

**12:00 A.M.**

Suddenly the clock in the church tower sounded twelve o'clock. Longingly, the cuckoo looked at his own clock. It crackled softly. Then it rattled. Then— the little door sprang open! The cuckoo couldn't believe his eyes. He leaped onto the clock. "Cuckoo!" he cried. "Cuckoo! Cuckoo!" exactly twelve times.

Everyone in the family woke up.

"The cuckoo is back!" shouted Susi.

"It's the cuckoo!" yelled Peter.

"The cuckoo!" cried Mother and Father.

As they all rushed downstairs to the kitchen, the man in the hat quickly jumped out the window (right into the flowerpot) and ran away.

When the family stood in front of the clock, they weren't sure if they had really heard it strike the hour or if they had dreamed it.

The cuckoo was so happy to be home that he decided to cuckoo an extra time. He popped out of the little door, flapped his wooden wings, and proudly called out "Cuckoo!" a thirteenth time. Then he slipped back inside and closed the door tightly behind him.

## About the Author

ANNEGERT FUCHSHUBER knew from the time she was a small girl that she wanted to be a children's book illustrator. "I want to make good books," she says, "books just as good as I can make them. But I am not trying to make the ultimate picture book. There is no such thing. Just as adults read the works of many different authors, children need many different pictures and books in order to become well-rounded and satisfied and eventually (and this is important!) to find their own taste."

Ms. Fuchshuber lives in West Germany with her family.